My Dad is Braver than your Dad.

Written By: Craig Hazen

Dedicated to-

To all the wonderful educators, motivators and parents of the world.

It was 'parent's day' in class and all the children were very excited to introduce the best and bravest adults in their lives.

Izzy sat in her desk patiently as all the others drew pictures of their parents. When she looked around at the desks, she could see that every parent was different. Some had different uniforms, business clothes, and some even looked like they had costumes on. She had not known there were so many things an adult could be.

Everyone's pictures looked finished, except for Izzy's.

A child looked at the blank page and exclaimed. "You haven't drawn anything!"

"It's a surprise," Izzy said.

"Well, whatever other parents do, they are not as brave as *my* dad!" A boy said, crossing his arms.

"Oh, ya?" Izzy asked.

"Ya!" A few students mumbled amongst themselves.

It seemed like everyone had the bravest parent, but they were about to find out once and for all...

Sophie was the first girl to present her parent. She showed a picture of a man in a big yellow suit with giant boots.

"My dad is braver than yours because he is a fireman. He puts out fires and sometimes goes into burning houses!" Sophie said proudly.

Izzy said, "Well, mine knows how to calm down fiery parents!"

The children looked at her.

What kind of job does that?

Sarah was next. She showed her dad with a big white coat around him. The best part was that he was holding a puppy!

"My dad is braver than yours for being a veterinarian," Sarah grinned.

"He protects and helps the animals, no matter how fierce they are!" she said

"Well, mine raises little heroes and feeds their imaginations," Izzy said, feeling proud.

The children looked at her again.
What kind of job does that?

Sean was the next to present his father. He showed his picture and Izzy knew exactly what his father was. The blue uniform and the shiny badge were immediate giveaways.

Sean said with pride in his voice, "My dad is braver than yours because he is a policeman. He stops bad guys and he gets to drive as fast as he wants!"

"Well, *mine* would jump in front of bullets if it was necessary," Izzy said.

The children looked at her once more.

What kind of job does that?

David brought out his paper in front of the class and everyone smiled and laughed.

"My dad is braver than yours because he has to make people laugh as a circus trainer. Sometimes that's hard to do," David explained.

"Well, *mine* has to entertain hundreds of children and sometimes it *feels* like a circus," Izzy told the class.

The children were once again surprised.
What kind of job does that?

Next, Kaitlin brought up her drawing. It was of a man standing on a stage with a bunch of people gathered around him.

"My dad is the bravest because he is a singer and he can perform in front of a thousand people!"

Izzy said proudly, "Well, *mine* has to show people how to have their *own* voice and be heard."

Now the children were even more confused. What kind of job could do that?

Michael walked up to the front of the class and showed his drawing. It was of a man jumping out of an airplane with a big red parachute.

"My dad is braver because he is a sky diving instructor and he can jump from any height!"

"Well, *mine* helps those who *are* afraid, to jump into their work and catches them when they fall." Izzy smiled as she spoke

Once again, the children had no idea.
What kind of job does that?

Another girl came up and drew her dad surrounded by lots of animals. There were giraffes, tigers, even rhinos in the picture.

"My dad is braver because he works in a zoo with wild animals!" the girl said.

"Well, *mine* works with wild *children*. I think that is much worse," Izzy said with a bright smile.

The children laughed, but still...
What kind of job does that?

The last boy came up and showed his father wearing goggles and standing next to a bunch of vials and tubes.

"My dad is the bravest because he is a chemist. He has to keep things from blowing up!"

Everyone gasped...

"Well, *mine* blows things up on purpose, like ideas and dreams," Izzy said with a grin.

Now the class had heard enough.

"What kind of job does that?!" they shouted.

They kept looking at Izzy's blank piece of paper, wondering if she had parents at all.

"Izzy, what does your dad do?!" one of her classmates asked.

Izzy got up from her desk and went to the front of the class just when there was a soft knock on the door.

"Funny you should ask... because my *mum* just so happens to be here." Izzy opened the door and once the children saw her, they knew exactly what kind of job did all those things.

"She's a school principal!" Izzy grinned.

Everyone clapped for Izzy's mum, because if what Izzy said was true, it meant that being a school principal was like being a fireman, policeman, zookeeper, veterinarian and chemist all in one. It must take true bravery to be a school principal if it meant being all those things at once.

Izzy was proud to present her mother to the class.

Although every child truly had brave parents in their own way, Izzy would always believe that hers was the best and bravest.

The End

CPSIA information can be obtained
at www.ICGtesting.com
Printed in the USA
LVHW070846270820
664258LV00003B/69

9 780648 928713